THE SANTASAURUS

By Mary Sheldon

Illustrated by Bartt Warburton
and Rick Penn-Kraus

For Elizabeth and Rebecca—
how did a mama get so lucky?
—M.S.

For Shirley, as always,
and for my other guiding lights—Flo, Sally, and Wu Lon.
Also, and most especially, for Cleo.
—B.W.

ISBN: 0-7871-0470-1

Printed in the United States of America

A Dove Kids Book
A Division of Dove Audio
8955 Beverly Boulevard
West Hollywood, CA 90048

Distributed by Penguin USA

Design by Rick Penn-Kraus

Type design and layout by Carolyn Wendt

First Printing: October 1996

10 9 8 7 6 5 4 3 2 1

The first thing the tiny dinosaur saw was the big man's face sparkling above him. And the first thing he felt was the big man's mittens pulling him out of the rough burlap bag and placing him in something warm and stretchy and red.

"You're going to be Robby's," the man said gently.

None of this made any sense to the tiny dinosaur. Who was this big man? Who was Robby? Who was *he*? He felt confused, shy, and frightened all at once.

With a little whimper, he hid his green cloth head under his stumpy front paw.

The big man laughed. "It's all right," he said. "You can take your head out and look."

The tiny dinosaur took his head out and looked.

What he saw was the small dark living room of a small dark apartment.

"This is where Mrs. McDermott and her son, Robby, live," the big man informed him.

The little dinosaur studied the place carefully.

Mrs. McDermott had tried to make the apartment look pretty, but—with her job at the bakery and raising Robby on her own—she didn't have much time or much money to spare. And so there were rips in the wallpaper, and chips in the paint, and holes in the furniture.

The little dinosaur, being new to the world, didn't see or understand a lot of the details. To him, it just seemed that everything around him was gloomy and sad.

But there was one thing about the room he entirely approved of. It was the big green good-smelling, prickly-looking thing in the corner. How bright and beautiful it was, covered with fascinating little balls and cones. The little dinosaur wished he knew what this magical thing was called. Almost, it seemed—he could remember; but not quite. *Royal Lizard!* he thought. How confusing everything was! He felt like crying, and once again he covered his eyes with his paw.

"It's called a tree," the big man reminded him. "And you're a Christmas toy in a little boy's stocking."

A tree? the little dinosaur thought in wonder. *A stocking? A toy?*

"Don't you remember?"

But the dinosaur did not remember, and he shook his head in shame.

The big man stroked him gently.

"It's Christmas Eve, a very powerful time. Make a wish, and I will grant it."

"A wish—I wish . . . I wish . . . I wish I could remember where I came from."

And then, suddenly, there was a melting, dizzying, whirring, stretching feeling. Everything seemed to fade away all at once. The little dinosaur closed his eyes. And when he opened them again, everything had disappeared—the sad room, the beautiful tree, the soft red stocking, and even the big man.

He found himself in a big steamy jungly-swamp.

The little dinosaur blinked in awed amazement. What an incredible place it was. The sky was a deep reddish color, and the earth was covered by moist and fragrant trees. And what sounds! Huge thumping footsteps . . . loud cawings . . . branches being broken.

What was happening?

Then the little dinosaur looked up and gasped. For there, all around him, were other dinosaurs; dozens and dozens of them—and all different. Some had big scales on their backs. Others had spikes on their tails. Some even flew through the air. *Royal Lizard!* the little dinosaur thought anxiously. They all looked so huge—bigger than the whole of the McDermott's apartment—and so fierce!

But then he happened to look across a clearing in the jungly-swamp, and he saw something that made all his fear go away. For there, smiling merrily at him, was another little dinosaur, just his size. She was absolutely lovely. Her skin was bronzed green, like a tree tinged with sunset. But it was her eyes that the little dinosaur most noticed. They were a deep, rich gold, and they flashed with such devilish mischief that he felt like laughing out loud.

Eagerly, the little dinosaur started to move toward her. But then, to his great disappointment, the melting, whirring, dizzying, stretching feeling came over him again.

And in just a moment he was back in the McDermott's apartment; back in Robby's Christmas stocking.

"Please, let me go back!" he begged the big man. "That other place is where I belong—not here."

The big man only smiled at him.

"I'm sorry, little one," he said softly. "You have things to do here."

The next morning was Christmas morning. When the sun rose, a small boy with curly blond hair and glasses came running into the room. When he saw his stocking, he grabbed it down eagerly and peered into it. Then, with a gasp of delight, he pulled out the little dinosaur.

"Mama! Mama! Look what Santa Claus brought me!"

Santa Claus . . . The little dinosaur smiled to himself. He had just learned who the big man had been.

"It's a dinosaur. He's an Apatosaurus, so I'm going to name him Pato."

The little dinosaur smiled again. He had just learned who *he* was.

From the first instant, Robby fell in love with his new toy.

"I'm going to hug him forever!" he told his mother happily.

Alas, this didn't exactly come as good news to Pato, since Robby had a habit of holding him so tightly around the stomach that Pato could feel his side seams meet!

That morning, after the rest of the Christmas presents had been opened, Robby showed Pato all over the apartment. And in the afternoon he showed Pato all around the building.

He took Pato upstairs and showed him where the Schumachers lived, and the Fazios, and Mrs. Lee, and Miss Stone. He took him downstairs and showed him where the McKenzies lived, and the O'Malleys, and the Slades, and the Rosens. Then he took him back to his own floor and showed him where the Sanchezes lived, and the Hansens, and Mr. Vine.

And then, finally, he took Pato outside and introduced him to the street and the neighborhood.

Pato didn't think much of the apartment, the building, the street, or the neighborhood. It looked so gloomy and dark to him. And the people all looked so sad. The ones they passed in the building had anxious frowns on their faces, and ones on the street were walking so fast and so stiffly.

Pato sighed. How he missed his jungly-swamp. And how he missed the beautiful little dinosaur with the mischievous golden eyes.

But there was nothing he could do about it. So he stayed unhappily in Robby's happy hand all day.

Robby had gotten another special present that morning. It was a book called *The Night Before Christmas*, and that evening his mother read it aloud to him.

Pato also listened, and as the story went on, he began to get very excited. For it was all about his friend Santa Claus—the big man who could do such wonderful magic.

So Pato listened hard to the poem—and he listened hard to what Robby's mother said about it afterwards.

She said that Santa Claus was the spirit of giving and love. And that love was the most powerful thing in the universe.

Pato nodded to himself. He knew how powerful Santa Claus was—even more powerful than those giant dinosaurs in the jungly-swamp! For hadn't Santa Claus been able to grant him his wish last night?

But what Pato *hadn't* realized was that Santa's power had come from giving and love.

And that's when the little dinosaur got his idea.

I'll become just like Santa Claus! Pato thought excitedly. *I'll start being loving and giving, too; and then I'll become just as powerful as he is. It won't take me long, I'm sure! And I'll be able to grant my own wish—and I'll wish to be back in the jungly-swamp forever, with that beautiful little Apatosaurus with the golden eyes.*

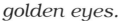

He decided to start his campaign the following day.

But it wasn't so easy. All morning long, Robby never let Pato out of his sight. The little dinosaur was getting very impatient—not to mention sore from all that squeezing! Then, luckily, after lunch, some boys from across the street tapped on the apartment door, wondering if Robby could come out to play.

His mother said yes—but told Robby that he'd better not take Pato with him. The little dinosaur might get dirty or hurt.

Sadly, Robby agreed. He kissed Pato six times—twice on the nose (did that ever tickle!), once on each cheek, once on each eyelid—and laid him gently on the bed.

"I'll walk down with you," his mother said. "I need to go to the store and buy some groceries."

The moment the door closed behind them, Pato got down to business.

The first thing to do was to find *The Night Before Christmas* again. He had seen where Robby's mother had put it, on a big shelf in the living room—"a . . . a bookshelf," she had called it. Pato craned his long neck back and looked up into the dizzying array of books above him. Ah! There it was!

He crawled first onto a footstool, then made his way onto a desk chair, and then managed to get onto the top of the desk. A short leap took him over to the bookcase. Carefully, he started to climb up the volumes to the shelf where the book was. His tiny front paws weren't much help, and his tail tended to get in the way, but at last he made it.

He reached *The Night Before Christmas* and put his paws carefully around it. He pulled as gently as he could, but the book came out faster than Pato expected. With a crash, down tumbled Pato, down tumbled the book, and down tumbled the five other volumes on either side.

Royal Lizard! thought Pato. He felt himself all over to see if anything were broken, but luckily there's not a whole lot that can happen to a toy stuffed dinosaur.

And at least he had *The Night Before Christmas*.

Eagerly, Pato opened the book and looked through it. He was able to figure out what most of the words were, because he had heard the poem once already. (Luckily for him, dinosaurs have extremely good memories.)

And then, carefully, he began to study all the pictures of Santa Claus.

But the more Pato looked, the more uncertain he became. And, finally, he gave a huge sigh and put the book down. *It's hopeless,* he thought sadly. He had to be honest with himself. There was no way around it. With his long tail and green body, he looked absolutely nothing like the big man in the white beard.

Let's face it, he thought miserably. *I'm never going to be Santa Claus.*

But what else could he be?

And then his glance fell upon another book—one of the ones that had crashed down on him from the bookcase. This one was called *The World of Dinosaurs.*

Pato began to look through it. And as he did, his spirits rose again. For there it was, that wonderful jungly-swamp; and there were all the dinosaurs he had seen last night—walking, flying, and swimming. And finally, there, too, was the dinosaur that looked like him—the noble Apatosaurus.

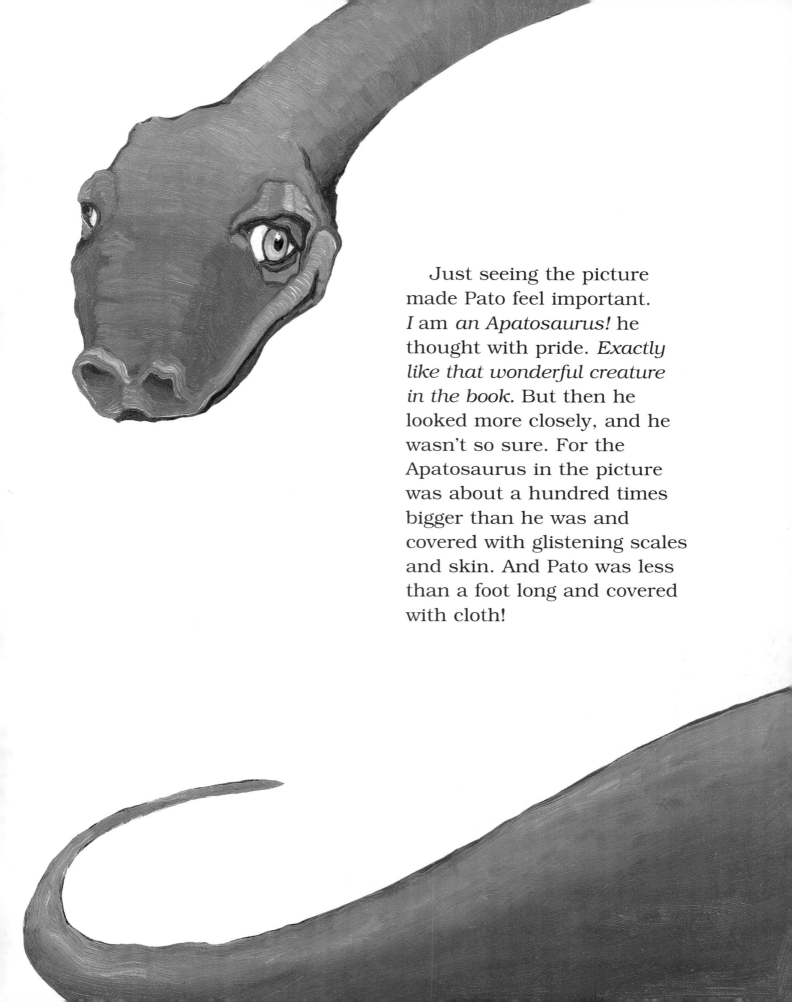

Just seeing the picture
made Pato feel important.
I am *an Apatosaurus!* he
thought with pride. *Exactly
like that wonderful creature
in the book.* But then he
looked more closely, and he
wasn't so sure. For the
Apatosaurus in the picture
was about a hundred times
bigger than he was and
covered with glistening scales
and skin. And Pato was less
than a foot long and covered
with cloth!

For a moment, Pato felt depressed again. But
then a wonderful thought occurred to him.
*So what if the Apatosaurus in the book has
glistening scales and skin?* he asked himself.
Glistening scales and skin weren't everything! It
didn't have cute button eyes like he did, or a
red stitched mouth, or green painted eyelashes!
It's okay, Pato thought with satisfaction.
*We're the same and yet we're different. And
neither one is better or worse than the other.
We're both special!*
Happy again, he went on with the book.
He saw pictures of the Stegosaurus, the
Ichthyosaurus, the Allosaurus, and the
Tyrannosaurus.
Isn't it interesting, Pato thought, *that
so many of the dinosaurs' names end
with "saurus."*
And then he gave a sudden
little yelp.
"That's it! That's it! I won't be
Santa Claus, after all! I'm a
dinosaur, and I'll be something
even better—I'll be the one and
only *Santasaurus!*"

Pato felt very pleased with himself indeed. For a minute or two, he paraded the room, simply basking in the glory of his new idea. But he was a practical dinosaur and soon got back to work. For even as Santasaurus, he decided, he still had to look the part. And what he needed, he knew, was a really terrific Santa skin.

So he went back to the *Night Before Christmas* book and studied Santa's costume carefully: red-and-white hat, white beard, red suit, black belt. *Royal Lizard!* Where on earth was he going to find those things?

Pato began to search the apartment.

I'll try to find the hat and beard first, he decided.

He looked everywhere, but Santa Claus hats and beards aren't easily found. The closest he got was a red paper cup for the hat and a ripped-off bit of tissue paper for the beard. But they felt so uncomfortable that he took them off.

And then, just as he was about to give up, he happened to look up on the mantelpiece—and he gasped with joy.

It should be mentioned here that Robby's mother had an older sister named Elizabeth. This sister Elizabeth was a clever woman, full of clever ideas. And that Christmas she had made an especially wonderful present. It was a bottle of wine, dressed up to look like Santa Claus. She had covered most of the bottle in red foil paper, given it felt arms and legs, and pasted on a paper belt and buttons. There was even a little burlap bag on the back. But the part that excited Pato was what she had done with the top of the bottle, for she had outfitted it with a perfect little felt Santa hat, complete with pom-pom, and under the neck of the bottle there was a fluffy cotton beard.

Pato was delighted. He felt badly about spoiling the decoration, but he knew he needed it in order to do his job.

With a bound, he jumped up to the mantelpiece and removed the hat and the beard.

And now for the Santa skin itself. Pato wished he could wrap himself up in red foil, like the bottle of wine, but his tail made this impossible. So another plan had to be found.

He went through the toy chest and looked through Robby's toys. He found a few soldiers, some stuffed animals, and finally, just when he was losing hope, he found a doll with a big S on its chest, a gold belt, and a red long thing that hung from its shoulders. For a moment, Pato was puzzled, and then he figured it out.

Wings! he thought happily. Kind of like a Pterodactyl's—only in one piece; and, thank goodness, a lot softer.

Pato was delighted. Just the thing! He felt a little guilty about taking the big red wing without Robby's permission, but he knew he could always put it back if he needed to.

Pato tried the wing on. He felt a little silly, with the edges of the fabric flopping around the floor, but he wasn't too discouraged. He was sure that, once he found something to put around his middle, it would be fine.

But what could he use?

One last time Pato went around the apartment. He tried on a green Christmas ribbon, but it had a sharp edge and hurt his soft stomach. He tried on a piece of yarn, but it was prickly and made him sneeze. And then, in the wastebasket, he found the perfect thing. Pato didn't know what it was, but Robby's mother would have recognized it as her old vacuum cleaner belt. It was black and made of plastic, and it fit perfectly around Pato's waist. Trembling with anticipation, he put on the belt and started to tuck his costume inside.

But was he in for trouble!

The first time Pato tried to fit everything together, all the fabric drooped to the left. The second time he tried, all the fabric drooped to the right. The third time he tried, all the fabric flopped over his tail and knocked him backwards.

Then Pato got mad. He glared at the red wing. He seized it in his paw, and he seized it in his teeth. In frustration, he began to tuck and pull and twist—and the next thing he knew, he was flat on his back, with the fabric wound tightly around his neck and his four feet stuck in the vacuum cleaner belt!

But he didn't give up. Not Pato! And, thanks to his perseverance, he finally succeeded. No matter that it was on the twenty-seventh try—he did it!

Proudly, he draped the material evenly around him, fitted the belt snugly, and stalked around the room.

I am the great Santasaurus, Pato thought. *I fear nothing.* And then he looked up—and screamed! For he had seen something—something scary . . . something green-and-red . . . something moving toward him!

Pato leaped straight in the air. He jumped back behind the bed. He trembled there for a minute, and then he stopped and peeked slowly out.

He had to find out what he had seen.

The creature also peeked out. It looked as scared as he did. Pato stared at it. It stared at him. Slowly, Pato went up to it. He put out his paw. The creature also put out its paw. *Well, at least he's friendly,* Pato thought. He touched the creature's paw, but to his surprise, he couldn't feel anything but a cold glassy surface.

At first, Pato was very puzzled. Then he began to look, not at the creature, but at the things that surrounded it. A bed—just like the one that was behind Pato himself. A chair—just like the one that was next to Pato. A carpet—just like the one that Pato was stepping on. A blue shoe on the floor—just like the one by Pato's own paws.

Pato thought hard. And when dinosaurs think hard, they usually come up with pretty good answers.

Royal Lizard! Pato thought with awe. For he now understood that the creature he was looking at was none other than himself.

Himself! Pato stepped back and took a better look. He looked from all angles. He looked from all sides.

Tears of pride and excitement filled Pato's eyes. What he was seeing in the mirror wasn't any old dinosaur. What he was seeing was—*Santasaurus himself!*

For a moment, Pato lost himself in the wonderful feeling. But soon he got practical again.

It was terrific that he looked like Santasaurus. But simply looking the part wasn't enough. After all, the real Santa Claus hadn't gotten to be powerful by simply changing his skin. His power had come through giving and love.

So, how can I be giving and loving? Pato wondered.

He figured it would be a good idea to start right where he was.

Pato looked around the apartment. It really was a pretty sad sight. What could a Santasaurus do to help the place out?

Well, for one thing, there was still a lot of Christmas trash lying around from the day before. Robby's mother had been so busy that she hadn't had the chance to clean it up yet. There were boxes, wrapping paper, ribbons, and, of course, Pato's favorite—the green Christmas tree in the corner, filled with its little balls and cones. But even it looked kind of sad today, its sparkle gone.

Pato spent the rest of the afternoon tidying up. He gathered the boxes together and put all the wrapping paper in the biggest one. Then he jumped up and down on it until the paper was nice and crushed beneath his feet. In fact, it was so crushed that he could no longer get out of the box. That was a scary moment. But Santasauruses are not scared for long, and Pato found that by hurling himself against the side of the box, he could turn it over and escape.

Now I'll tidy up all this bright silver dangly stuff, he decided next.

Carefully, he swept all the tinsel into a neat pile. He wished he didn't have to throw it away; it was so terrifically shiny. Pato thought about hanging a few of the strands around his waist, to give his Santa skin a . . . a little extra flair; but it tripped him up. So, sadly, he had to abandon the idea.

Then, finally, when all the tidying was done, Pato was faced with the problem of what to do with the Christmas tree. He wasn't big enough to carry it downstairs to the trash, but he did the next best thing. First, he tied a paper bag to his tail. Then, taking off his belt, he slung it over the branches and used it as a rope to climb into the tree. And, inching his way up, he carefully climbed along the branches and unhooked each one of the shiny balls and cones. Gently, one by one, he placed them in the bag. And when it was filled, he let himself down to the ground again and returned the balls and cones to their boxes.

Since his bag was tiny, he had to make many journeys up and down the tree. And by the time he finished, he was exhausted.

But it's worth it, Pato thought. *I'm a little closer to being Santa Claus, and a little closer to getting back to my jungly-swamp and the dinosaur with the twinkling golden eyes.*

But his sense of peace did not last long. Because, suddenly, Pato heard footsteps coming down the hall. Someone was coming! Frantically, he dashed for Robby's bedroom. Frenziedly, he tore off his Santa skin. Wildly, he plucked off his beard and hat. Crazedly, he threw everything in the lowest bureau drawer, behind where he had seen Robby put his pajamas. Then, panting, he raced back into the living room and hurled himself onto the sofa. And by the time Robby came home again, Pato was lying back on the pillow, exactly as the little boy had left him, looking just like an ordinary stuffed toy. Except that, if Robby had peeked very closely, he would have seen Pato's chest heaving up and down!

A few moments later, Robby's mother also came home. When she saw the living room all cleaned up, she gave a little cry of surprise.
"Did you do this, Robby?"
But Robby said he hadn't.
"Maybe it was Santa Claus."
Pato couldn't help smiling.

That night, he dreamed about the jungly-swamp again—the hot, deep, mysterious jungly-swamp. And there she was—the beautiful little Apatosaurus with the twinkling golden eyes. This time, Pato found the courage to go up to her.

"Hello," he said shyly.

"Hello, big guy," she answered, not shyly at all. "I've wanted to talk to you, but you keep comin' and goin'."

Her voice was wonderful—husky and low—just like Pato had secretly hoped it would be.

"One of these days, I'll be here to stay," he told her earnestly. "I'm just not sure how long it's going to take."

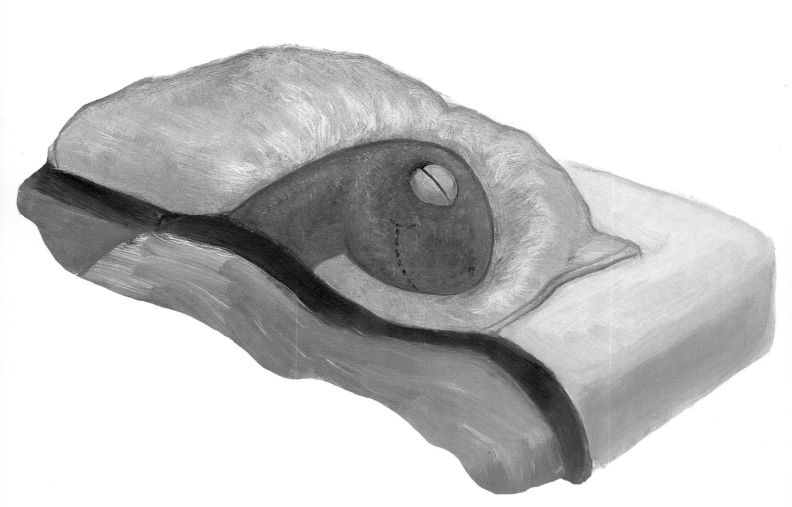

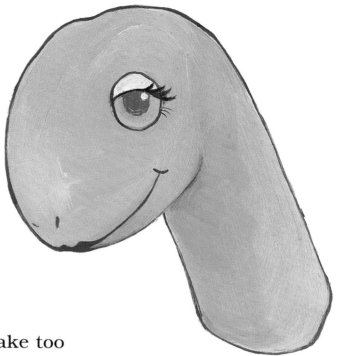

　　"Well, see that it doesn't take too long," she answered. "I know we dinosaurs live a long time, but I haven't got a million years to wait, y'know."

　　And she winked at him with one twinkly golden eye.

　　Pato couldn't sleep at all for the rest of the night. He kept reliving the moment, over and over in his mind. That wink . . . those eyes . . . that voice!

　　Yes, there was no doubt about it. He had to get back to the jungly-swamp as fast as he could.

The weeks went by, and winter turned to spring. The small, scraggly trees planted amidst the concrete sidewalks began to bloom, and window gardens full of crocuses and daffodils brightened the drab brick buildings. Seeing all the green around him made Pato miss his jungly-swamp all the more.

He was Santasaurus every day. Each morning, as soon as Robby left for day care, and his mother left for her job at the bakery, Pato changed into his Santa skin.

By this time, he was excellent at speed-dressing. Those early days, in which it had taken him twenty-seven tries to get his Santa skin arranged, were a distant memory. Nowadays, he was getting so good that he started timing himself to see if he could beat his own record. One proud April day, he actually changed into his Santa skin in less than thirty seconds. (Human time, that is; if you count it in dinosaur time, it's thirty days, but either way, it's an impressive score.)

And then he began his work.

The first thing Pato did was spend an hour getting helpful information for his daily Santasaurus deed. This he got from the big bookcase in the living room.

Pato had gotten very fond of the bookcase. Every morning he would crawl up into it and choose a different book. Robby's mother loved to read, and there were plenty of choices.

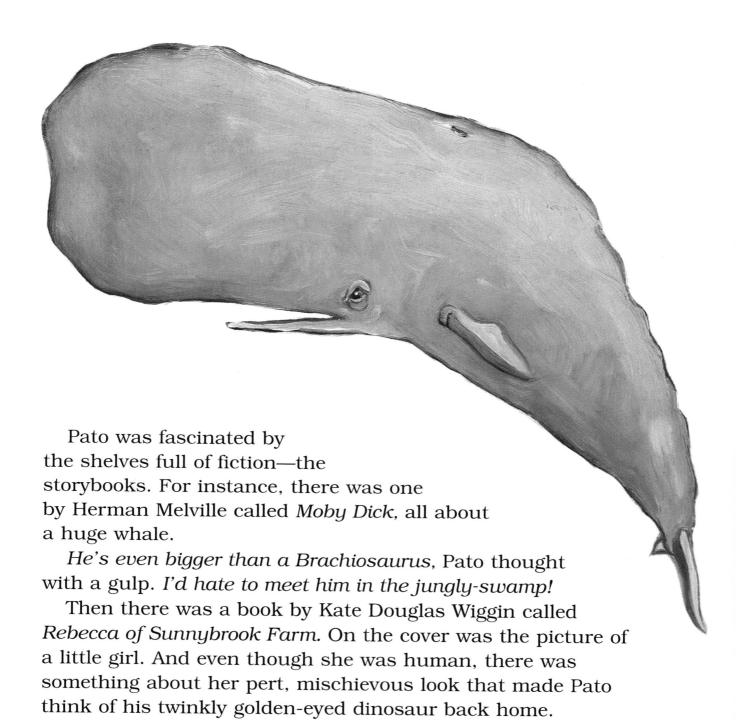

Pato was fascinated by
the shelves full of fiction—the
storybooks. For instance, there was one
by Herman Melville called *Moby Dick,* all about
a huge whale.

He's even bigger than a Brachiosaurus, Pato thought
with a gulp. *I'd hate to meet him in the jungly-swamp!*

Then there was a book by Kate Douglas Wiggin called
Rebecca of Sunnybrook Farm. On the cover was the picture of
a little girl. And even though she was human, there was
something about her pert, mischievous look that made Pato
think of his twinkly golden-eyed dinosaur back home.

In addition to all the storybooks, there were also shelves full of nonfiction books—books with facts in them: cookbooks, books on growing flowers, books on how to amuse children on rainy days. But Pato had three favorites. The first was called *The Way Things Work,* which answered a lot of questions he had—everything from the way the stars moved across the heavens at night to the way the dishwasher got the dishes clean. The second was called *365 Ways to Save the Earth,* which was full of hints for rescuing the ecology. Pato was very concerned about the ecology. The thought of living in a world where trees and plants were being destroyed daily made him tremble. *I wish I could be Santasaurus to all the plants and trees,* he thought wistfully.

And lastly, most useful to Pato, was a particularly wonderful book called *How to Fix Just About Anything.* And Pato would read and read.

Then, after an hour or so, he was ready to be Santasaurus.

Every day he did something loving and giving. One day he sewed a button onto Robby's mother's jeans (page 37 of *How to Fix Just About Anything*).

Another day he took a roll of paper towels and washed all the windows (page 34l). Tails, Pato discovered, make excellent window washers. Except for the time he got so carried away that he ended up doing a back flip!

Another day he hunted around the whole apartment until he found that special aggie marble Robby had lost.

Another day he drew Robby a picture of dinosaurs, using every single crayon in the box. He went wild with creativity and gave his Pterodactyl a polka-dot body, his Stegosaurus a pink-and-green striped skin, and his Apatosaurus, naturally, shimmering golden eyes. Pato considered the picture a masterpiece.

Until, that is, Robby brought it in to show his mother.

"What a lovely painting!" she said. "A flower garden in full bloom."

Pato spent most of the next morning reading a book entitled *How to Paint—in Twelve Easy Lessons.*

But perhaps the most memorable day was the day that Pato decided to do the family laundry.

At first, everything went beautifully. Pato felt very proud of himself as he loaded in the clothes and put in the detergent.

I am the great Santasaurus, and nothing is too difficult for me! he hummed softly to himself.

But, alas, there's an old expression: "Pride goeth before a fall." And just as Pato was lifting the lid of the washing machine and adding the fabric softener to the last rinse (p. 381 of *How to Fix Absolutely Anything*), he slipped on the detergent and fell with a huge splash into the washing machine!

It was not a great experience. Pato whirled around, soapy and dizzy. And by the time he finally hauled himself out, he barely had time to squeeze himself dry before Robby and his mother came home. But, at least, Pato thought gloomily, the fabric softener had certainly done its job. His skin had never felt better.

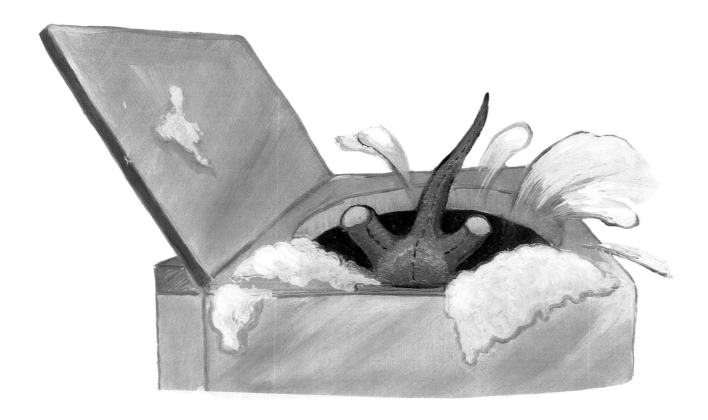

As time went on, Pato got more and more used to his life in the apartment. Of course, he told himself he didn't really belong there. But until the day came when he could go back to the jungly-swamp and the beautiful little Apatosaurus who lived there, it wasn't really so bad being where he was, or being with the people he was with. In fact, he didn't even mind it so much nowadays when Robby hugged him too hard around the middle. Except for that one time Robby's hug was so strong that Pato's button eyes flew off and had to be sewn back on!

Robby continued to adore Pato. He slept with him every night and started every day by giving him his six kisses: the two incredibly tickly ones on the nose, one on each cheek, and one on each eyelid.

And even Robby's mother, busy as she was, made Pato feel important. "One day when I have time, I'll sew him a little jacket," she told her son. "Wouldn't he look cute in a costume?"

If only she knew! Pato thought with a secret smile. *If only she knew!*

But she never knew. And neither did Robby. Neither of them could ever figure out who it was who washed the dishes, or fixed the toaster, or wrote the amazing poem about Pterodactyls.

"I'm actually starting to believe in fairies!" Robby's mother said in bewilderment.

"I tell you, it's Santa Claus," Robby said wisely.

And once again Pato smiled.

Time went on. Easter passed, Mother's Day, and then it was summer. Every day Pato still did his Santasaurus deed; and every night he dreamed about the jungly-swamp, and the beautiful little Apatosaurus with the twinkling golden eyes and the adorably husky voice. How he missed her— everything about her: the delicate way she dipped her neck when she drank; the way she fluttered her eyelashes; the way she teased him. How he longed to be with her, but nothing was happening. Every day he would wish; and every day the wish didn't work. He still wasn't powerful enough. He still wasn't enough like Santa Claus.

One day Pato decided to branch out. Maybe it wasn't enough helping out Robby and his mother, he thought. Maybe he ought to try helping out other people, too.

So Pato began a new campaign: being Santasaurus for everyone in the apartment building.

He started with his own floor. Mr. and Mrs. Sanchez, the lovely couple who lived across the way, weren't having a good summer. The fan in their apartment wasn't working, and the place was terribly hot. Mr. Sanchez, especially, was uncomfortable in the heat.

Pato sneaked into their apartment one broiling July morning. It was easy to do. With the place so hot, they always left their front door open, hoping to get a breeze from the hall.

Mr. Sanchez was complaining about the heat.

"I'll go to the store and get you some more iced tea mix," his wife said. "Maybe that'll make you feel better."

When she left, Mr. Sanchez decided to take a nap. He fell asleep on the sofa. He never saw the tiny Santasaurus climbing onto the pillow beside him. Gently, Pato picked up a big geranium leaf and began to fan Mr. Sanchez. The old man smiled in his sleep. When Pato heard Mrs. Sanchez coming up the stairs, he quickly climbed down the sofa arm and hid in the dust ruffle.

That was perhaps a mistake. The ruffle lived up to its name and was about the dustiest place Pato had ever encountered. Dust flew into his eyes, up his nose—and suddenly, the little dinosaur felt a loud, enormous sneeze coming on!

Oh, no! he thought. *I've got to get out of here fast.*

Desperately, he lunged for the door, holding his nose. But the more he tried to be quiet, the worse things got. The floor squeaked! The rag rug rustled! And he almost knocked over the standing lamp.

But he finally made it. And as he sneaked out the front door, he heard Mrs. Sanchez say to her husband, "Well, you must have had a nice nap. You seem so much happier now."

"I am," he replied. "I was dreaming I was somewhere cold—the North Pole, maybe."

With Santasaurus! Pato thought with a grin. And then, when he was safely halfway down the hall . . . "Ah-choo!"

The sneeze was so strong, it blew him halfway down the hall!

The next day, Pato visited the other neighbors, the Hansens. There were six of them: a mother, father, and four little girls. They had all gone out to the beach for the day, leaving the apartment empty. It wasn't easy for Pato to get inside. There was only a space of a few inches between the closed door and the floor, and Pato had to squeeze as flat as he could. He got stuck twice, and as he pulled himself free, there was a sudden awful rip. His red wings had torn almost in two! Pato looked down at himself and sighed. At least, he told himself, he had accomplished his mission. He had gotten into the Hansens' apartment.

And now that he was there, what should he do for them?

He decided to make them some spaghetti sauce. Pato had never actually cooked before, but he had seen a recipe in Robby's mother's Italian cookbook which looked delicious. Pato's main worry was how he was going to lift the saucepan onto the stove, but luckily, there was a clean pan already there.

It was fun making the sauce. Pato found the jar of tomato paste in the larder, managed the can opener very well with his paws, and chose some beautiful onions and peppers from one of the big baskets the Hansens had hanging from the ceiling. Carefully, Pato chopped the vegetables, added salt and pepper, and stirred everything together. As a final touch, he picked some oregano from the miniature vegetable garden on the fire escape and sprinkled it on top of the mixture.

Pato had read that all great chefs sample their productions, and so, with a great flourish, he dipped his tail dramatically first into the sauce, and then into his mouth. But his flourish was perhaps a little too grand; or maybe it was that his tail was a little too large. But, whatever the reason, there was first a huge awful splash, followed by a warm wet wave—and the next thing Pato knew, he had covered himself, his Santa skin, and half the Hansens' kitchen with bright red spaghetti sauce. (Which, incidentally, was delicious.)

Pato groaned softly and looked sadly around the scene of destruction. But by the time the Hansens came back from the beach, the kitchen was sparkling clean once again, and the spaghetti sauce was simmering on the stove.

When Pato heard the key in the lock, he jumped hurriedly down from the counter.

Whoosh! His tiny paws slid across the kitchen floor, and he hid behind the larder door until the family had walked by into the living room.

"Good-bye," Pato whispered.

And then he thought that, since he had made them spaghetti sauce, it would be more proper to say good-bye in Italian.

"Ciao!"

And Pato giggled because he was so smart.

During the rest of the week, Pato made secret visits to every apartment in the building.

He visited the Schumachers, the elderly couple on the top floor. Since it was hard for them to bend over, Pato decided to wash their kitchen floor for them. He did it late one night when they were asleep and had a fine time, skating back and forth on a big bar of soap.

Then he visited the Slades' apartment. They were a father and his grown son who worked together in a family business. They loved plants but didn't have the time to care for them. So Pato spent one whole afternoon pruning their pots of ivy.

Next he visited the Mackenzies' apartment. They had a toddler who loved to tear up pieces of paper. So Pato made twenty-five paper dolls for her to enjoy.

For Mrs. Lee, the widow who lived alone, Pato wanted to do something special. Mrs. Lee, born in the Chinese countryside, was having a hard time adjusting to life in a big American city, and Pato wanted to make her feel more at home. One day, when he was browsing through the big bookcase, he saw a Chinese-American dictionary and got an idea. The following day, he left an elegant little note on Mrs. Lee's doorstep, which said "Have a nice day" in Chinese characters.

Pato lurked outside in the hall until he saw Mrs. Lee come out of her apartment. She picked up the note, read it, and burst into happy tears.

Pato pranced proudly away.

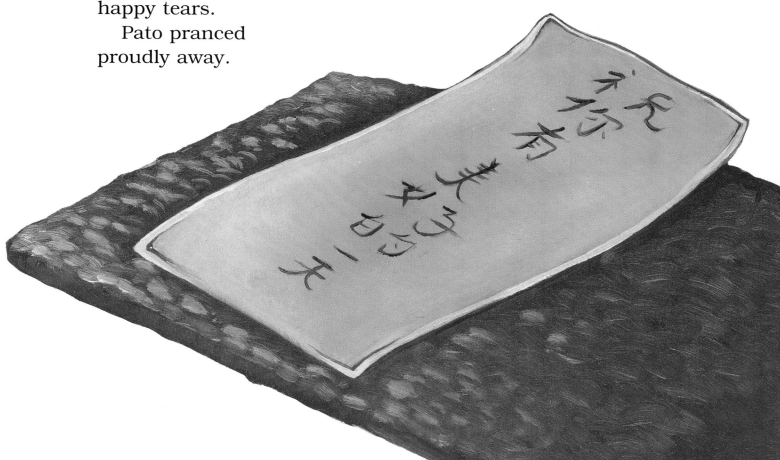

Royal Lizard! he thought as he went to sleep that night. *I certainly have gotten a lot of good use from that bookcase!*

Now, living in big cities isn't always easy. There's a lot of stress and noise, and sometimes people aren't as kind as they could be. This was the case with the people in Robby's building. Not that they weren't wonderful people, all of them, but they just weren't very friendly to one another. They said hello sometimes, when they passed each other in the hall, but that was about it.

But when Pato started his work as Santasaurus, all that began to change. And for the very first time, the people in the building actually started to talk to one another.

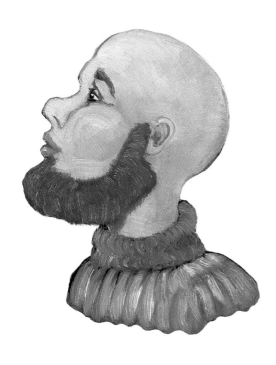

Mr. Vine and Miss Stone had passed each other in the lobby every day for twelve years, and in all that time, they had never exchanged more than a nod. But on this particular September day, when Mr. Vine came upon Miss Stone going out the front door, he felt so curious that he had to speak.

"Excuse me," he said. "This may sound crazy to you, but have you noticed anything strange going on in your apartment lately?"

"Strange?" she asked.

"Yes. Mysterious. Like dishes being washed, and nobody being there to wash them. Like pants being hemmed, and nobody being there to hem them."

"Why, yes!" Miss Stone said. "As a matter of fact, just last night, I came in and found my flats of pansies had been mysteriously transplanted!"

Mr. Vine looked at her with interest.

"You grow pansies?" he asked. "That happens to be a hobby of mine, also!"

And off they went, talking like friends, for the first time in twelve years.

Pato happened to be in the corridor, and he heard the conversation. He couldn't help smiling.

Soon, all the neighbors in the building were talking; talking about the mystery of the unknown helper. One day they even held a big meeting to try and figure out what was going on.

Since Robby and his mother were at the meeting, Pato went along, too, squeezed in Robby's hand. He enjoyed himself very much. It was fun hearing the tenants talk about the things he had done for them. But nobody had any idea who was responsible, or how this person got into their apartments—or out of them.

"It's Santa Claus," little Robby kept saying. "I tell you, it's Santa Claus."

But of course the adults didn't listen to him.

Pato kept on with his busy schedule. By the time October came, he was exhausted. He looked in the mirror one day, and the sight depressed him. He was getting too thin, and the fur on his forepaws was rubbing off. Also, his Santasaurus skin was a mess. His beard was ragged, and his red wings were in tatters.

This is ridiculous, Pato thought. *I'm going to have to cut down.*

So he made himself a schedule. Every day, in addition to helping Robby and his mother out, he decided to be Santasaurus for only one other family in the building. He put all the families' names down on a list and visited them all in strict rotation, alphabetically. This way, at least, he could catch up on his sleep; and dream a little more about his jungly-swamp and the lovely little dinosaur. *Those twinkly golden eyes,* Pato thought longingly. *That husky voice . . . those fluttering eyelashes . . . the way she dips her neck . . . and*—the latest thing he had noticed about her—*those delicate feet with those three adorable toes . . .*

"So when are you going to be here for always?" she would ask him every time they saw each other. "I grant you, you're worth waitin' for, but I should warn you—patience was never my greatest virtue!" But she fluttered her lashes so outrageously as she said it that Pato's feelings didn't get hurt.

"I'll be here as soon as I can," he told her. "It's almost Christmas again. I've been Santasaurus for nearly a year now. I'm hoping I've gotten powerful enough so that when Christmas Eve comes, I can wish myself back to you forever and ever."

She nodded.

"Sounds good to me. Don't get too powerful, though. I still like to boss you around."

But then, at the beginning of December, something happened that, for a while, made everything else seem to fade away. What happened was that Robby got sick.

It started out as just an ordinary cold. But it soon got worse and worse. Robby's mother even took him to the doctor, but none of the medicines worked. For over two weeks, Robby lay in bed. His body felt hot. His eyes were glazed. He couldn't speak. He couldn't even breathe.

Pato was very frightened. He lay in the little boy's arms, hour after hour. It was awful to see Robby, usually so full of energy, now so still and weak.

Pato did everything he could. He bathed Robby's forehead with a cold towel and rubbed his legs. At first, he did everything when the little boy was asleep, for Pato still didn't want Robby to know that he was a real live dinosaur.

But then more days went by, and Robby got sicker and sicker. Suddenly, Pato's secret didn't seem so important anymore. And one day he jumped up onto Robby's pillow and told him the truth—that he was really Santasaurus.

Robby smiled and whispered, "I've always known."

Robby's mother took several days off from work to be with her son, but she knew she had to get back to the bakery soon, or she would lose her job. She sat in the living room one morning, wondering what she was going to do. There was a knock on her door, and she answered it. To her surprise, it was the upstairs neighbor, Mrs. Lee. She was carrying a pot of steaming wonton soup, and she smiled at Robby's mother.

"I heard your little boy was sick," she said shyly. "I wonder if you need some help in looking after him. My children are all grown, and it would be a pleasure to be with a child again."

Robby's mother took the soup, and the offer, with thanks. Just as she had recovered from the surprise, there was another knock at the door. This time it was Mr. Vine.

"I hear the kid is sick," he said gruffly. "I don't have anything better to do—how 'bout if I sit with him for a little while?" And he shoved a fistful of pansies at her.

Later that afternoon, four more neighbors came around, offering to look after Robby while his mother was at work.

Robby's mother burst into happy tears.

Things have sure changed around here, she thought. *A year ago, this never would have happened.*

Whenever Robby's mother or the neighbors were in the room, Pato pretended to be an ordinary stuffed toy. But whenever he and Robby were alone, they had a great time.

Pato played Candy Land with Robby,

read him his favorite sports books,

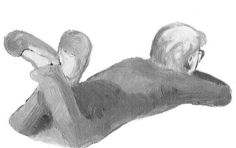

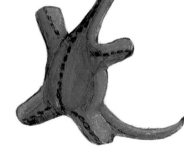

and told him stories about the wonderful world of the jungly-swamp.

Then, when Robby's mother came in, and Robby told her all the things he and Pato had done together, she just shook her head sadly and said the fever was making him imagine it.

One night the fever got so high that it looked as if Robby would have to go to the hospital.

Pato felt very sad and afraid. He lay in the little boy's arms and held him all night with his paws.

In the morning, when Pato woke up, Robby wasn't there. Where was he? Had he gotten worse? Had he been taken to the hospital? And then, to the little dinosaur's relief, he heard a familiar voice calling from the living room:

"Mama! Mama! Please, bring me Pato!"

Robby was better. His fever had broken in the night. He recovered very fast, and in a week he was completely well.

Once the fever was gone, Robby didn't remember much at all about being sick. He did remember—at least, he thought he remembered—that for a few days, his toy dinosaur had come alive. But when he spoke to his mother about it, she only laughed and said he must have imagined it. And soon, Robby began to think he had imagined it, too.

The days were very short now. Snow began to fall. And soon, it was Christmas Eve.

In the spirit of a true Santasaurus, Pato had been very busy preparing for this special night.

For weeks now, he had been secretly gathering up and filing magazine pictures. And now he made everyone in the building a big decorated card, filled with pictures of the things they most liked. The Schumachers' card had fast cars, Elvis Presley, and Van Gogh's "Starry Night" on it. Little Amy Fazio's card had pictures of kittens and baseball players. Miss Stone's card had travel pictures of France. And Mr. Vine's card had pansies and a picture of Betty Grable.

Pato signed them all "Love, Santa."

After dinner on Christmas Eve, Pato sneaked out and distributed his cards. No one in the building had been forgotten.

Then he came back to his apartment, excited beyond belief at the thought of what lay ahead.

At eight o'clock, it was time for Robby to go to bed.

"Hang up your stocking, darling. Maybe Santa Claus will come," his mother told him.

Robby hung up his stocking. Then he got into bed and held Pato beside him.

After Robby went to sleep, Pato crept out of the bed. He dressed quietly in his Santa skin and went into the living room.

His heart was thudding. He knew it was tonight, or never. But had he made himself powerful enough? Had he done enough this last year to wish himself back to the jungly-swamp?

He would soon find out.

At the first stroke of midnight, Pato knew it was time. He took a deep breath and made his wish. He wished as hard as he could.

I want to be back in the jungly-swamp; back with my golden-eyed dinosaur.

He felt the power growing within him, growing . . .

It's going to happen! It's going to happen!

But it didn't happen.

Pato opened his eyes. He was still in the apartment; still on the couch; still a stuffed dinosaur.

He held back wails of misery. Tears of disappointment ran down his fuzzy cheeks. He had failed. He had failed as a Santasaurus. And he had failed to make his dream come true.

Then, on the last stroke of twelve, a sudden flash of light filled the room. What was happening?! Fearfully, Pato hid his eyes. When he finally found the courage to open them, there stood Santa Claus.

Pato was awed and humbled. He had forgotten how big Santa Claus was—and how wise-looking. Standing there before the huge man, wearing his tattered red wings and drooping beard that by now had turned to a dark gray, Pato felt ashamed, and silly, and insignificant. For a moment, he even wondered if Santa Claus would be angry with him for what he had done.

But Santa Claus wasn't angry at all. He looked at Pato in such a kind and understanding way that the little dinosaur felt like crying.

"What's the matter?" Santa asked.

Out it all came. How, last Christmas, Santa Claus had given that special wish—and how Pato had seen the jungly-swamp he had come from. How he had fallen in love with the dinosaur with twinkly golden eyes, and longed to live with her forever; and how, in order to do that, he had tried to become powerful by being like Santa Claus all year long and helping everyone in the building.

"And then tonight I tried to grant my wish," Pato wailed. "But it didn't work! I just wasn't powerful enough."

Again the big man smiled. "There is more than one way of having power. You have no idea of the good you have done for these people here, or the many ways you have touched their lives. That is a very beautiful kind of power to have—perhaps the most beautiful kind of all. I have watched you all through the year, little Santasaurus, and I've been very proud of you. And so I *will* grant your heart's desire."

Pato's whole body filled with joy.

"Now, what is it that you want? You want to go back to the jungly-swamp—is that it? Live in prehistoric times, with the dinosaur with the twinkling golden eyes?"

"Yes!"

"I can do that for you. But there's one thing you must remember. If you go back there, you'll never be able to come back to this world again—not even in your dreams."

"Oh, that's all right—" Pato started to say, and then he stopped. For he suddenly remembered the touch of Robby's hand; even when he clutched him around the stomach too tightly.

Never to see Robby again?

And then a hundred other images began to rise before Pato. All the people he had helped as Santasaurus: Mrs. Lee, so delighted with her friendship card; the Slades' baby, settling back to sleep while he hummed her lullabyes;

the time he had made little Sarah Fazio an origami penguin; rolling up Mrs. Hansen's knitting wool;

finding Mr. Vine's glasses for the fiftieth time.

Tears filled his eyes, and Pato looked at Santa Claus in dismay.

Santa Claus smiled again. His smile was very tender.

"That's the danger in giving to people, Pato," he said. "When you give to someone, you generally end up loving them."

Pato didn't know what to do. He stared at Santa Claus in desperation.

"You have only a minute to decide," Santa Claus told him.

But Pato still couldn't make up his mind.

Then, finally, when there were only a few seconds left in the minute, he thought of Robby again: Robby's smile, Robby's laugh, and the way he had felt when Robby had gotten so sick.

And he knew he couldn't leave; not just yet.

"All right," Pato blurted out, "all right. I'll stay here one more year. Just one more year. Then, next Christmas, I'll go to the jungly-swamp, where I belong."

Santa laughed and laughed. The whole room seemed to be full of light; and then he disappeared.

Pato crawled under the sofa. He felt miserable, and small, and very, very foolish.

"It was my big chance! My only chance. And I ruined it. Now I'll never be with my beautiful dinosaur again."

And he put his head in his paws and cried.

The minute night turned into morning, Robby bounced into the living room.

"Merry Christmas!" he cried.

He picked Pato up and squeezed him, as usual, much too hard around the stomach.

And he gave him his six kisses: the two tickly ones on the nose, one on each cheek, and one on each eyelid.

"And since it's your birthday," Robby said, "I'm giving you an extra one!"

And he gave Pato a huge kiss on the top of the head.

Seeing Robby, seeing his eager warm face and feeling his kisses, Pato felt a little better.

And then, with a gasp, Robby caught sight of his Christmas stocking. Eagerly, he ran over and grabbed it down from the mantelpiece.

"Mama! Mama! Santa Claus did come! Oh, look—look what he's brought me."

Out of his red felt stocking he pulled a stuffed toy. It was a beautiful little dinosaur.

With one twinkly golden eye she winked at Pato.

"I got tired of waitin', big guy," she whispered.

Overcome with amazement and joy, Pato fell backwards off the sofa.

"Royal Lizard!" was all he could say.

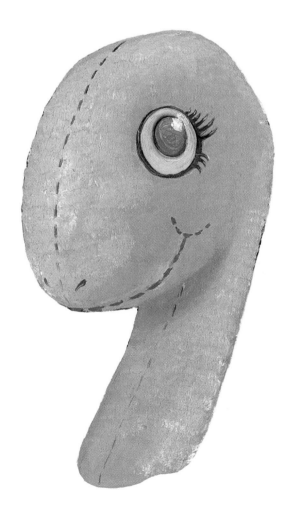